BUILDING BY DESIGN

ONE WORLD TRADE CENTER

BY CECILIA PINTO MCCARTHY

CONTENT CONSULTANT
Louis F. Geschwindner
Professor Emeritus of Architectural Engineering
The Pennsylvania State University

Core Library
An Imprint of Abdo Publishing
abdopublishing.com

Cover image: One World Trade center rises high above nearby buildings in Lower Manhattan, New York City.

abdopublishing.com

Published by Abdo Publishing, a division of ABDO, PO Box 398166, Minneapolis, Minnesota 55439. Copyright © 2018 by Abdo Consulting Group, Inc. International copyrights reserved in all countries. No part of this book may be reproduced in any form without written permission from the publisher. Core Library™ is a trademark and logo of Abdo Publishing.

Printed in the United States of America, North Mankato, Minnesota
032017
072018

THIS BOOK CONTAINS RECYCLED MATERIALS

Distributed in paperback by North Star Editions, Inc.

Cover Photo: Steve Heap/Shutterstock Images
Interior Photos: Steve Heap/Shutterstock Images, 1; Lisa Blue/iStockphoto, 4–5, 45; Andrew Burton/Getty Images News/Getty Images, 7, 16–17; Gary Hershorn/Corbis News/Getty Images, 8, 43; AP Images, 10; Shawn Baldwin/AP Images, 12–13; Allan Tannenbaum/Archive Photos/Getty Images, 15; Mario Tama/Getty Images News/Getty Images, 20, 27; Red Line Editorial, 22; Mark Lennihan/AP Images, 24–25; Jack Aiello/Shutterstock Images, 28; Roman Babakin/Shutterstock Images, 30; Drew Angerer/Getty Images News/Getty Images, 34–35; Spencer Platt/Getty Images News/Getty Images, 37, 39

Editor: Arnold Ringstad
Imprint Designer: Maggie Villaume
Series Design Direction: Laura Polzin

Publisher's Cataloging-in-Publication Data

Names: McCarthy, Cecilia Pinto, author.
Title: Engineering One World Trade Center / by Cecilia Pinto McCarthy.
Description: Minneapolis, MN : Abdo Publishing, 2018. | Series: Building by design | Includes bibliographical references and index.
Identifiers: LCCN 2016962133 | ISBN 9781532111631 (lib. bdg.) | ISBN 9781641852524 (pbk) | ISBN 9781680789485 (ebook)
Subjects: LCSH: Structural engineering--Miscellanea--Juvenile literature. | One World Trade Center (New York, N.Y.)--Design and construction--Juvenile literature. | Civil engineering--Juvenile literature. | New York (N.Y.)--Buildings, structures, etc.--Juvenile literature. | Buildings--Miscellanea--Juvenile literature. | Skyscrapers--New York (N.Y.)--Juvenile literature.
Classification: DDC 624--dc23
LC record available at http://lccn.loc.gov/2016962133

CONTENTS

CHAPTER ONE
One World Trade Center **4**

CHAPTER TWO
Preparing to Build a Tower **12**

CHAPTER THREE
**Building One World
Trade Center** **24**

CHAPTER FOUR
**One World Trade
Center Today** **34**

Fast Facts **42**

Stop and Think **44**

Glossary **46**

Learn More **47**

Index **48**

About the Author **48**

CHAPTER
ONE

ONE WORLD TRADE CENTER

The glass and stainless steel of One World Trade Center make the tower sparkle. The building rises into the blue sky as part of the Manhattan skyline. It stands 1,776 feet (541 m) from its base to the tip of its spire. This number is symbolic. It represents the year the nation's founders signed the Declaration of Independence. The tower soars above all other buildings in New York City. Nicknamed the Freedom Tower, it became the tallest skyscraper in the Western Hemisphere when completed.

One World Trade center sits among many other skyscrapers in Manhattan.

BUILDING BIGGER

During the late 1800s, cities became crowded with people. Space became expensive and scarce. Builders solved the problem by building taller buildings. The first skyscraper was built in Chicago in 1885. It had ten floors. Over time, new technology made it possible to build taller structures. By 2017 the world's tallest building was the Burj Khalifa. It is in Dubai, United Arab Emirates. The tower stands 2,716 feet (828 m) tall. It has 163 floors. The Burj Khalifa was designed by the same architecture firm that worked on One World Trade Center.

Skyscrapers are extremely tall buildings. Their dozens of floors are used for apartments or office space. One World Trade Center has 104 floors. It is one of five buildings in the 16-acre (6.5-ha) World Trade Center complex. At the building's base, water gently cascades down 30 feet (9.1 m) into two memorial pools. The pools mark the sites where the two former World Trade Center towers once stood. These buildings were called the Twin Towers. A terrorist attack destroyed them on September 11, 2001.

The huge memorial pools help visitors appreciate the enormous size of the former Twin Towers.

The planning and building of One World Trade Center was a long, complicated process. Construction began in 2006. The tower finally opened for business in 2014. One World Trade Center is a masterpiece of architecture and engineering. The building's square base is covered in angled pieces of glass. The structure

seems to twist as it rises into eight long triangles. The triangles form an octagon in the tower's cross section halfway up. At the roof, they form another square. A communications ring sits at the very top. It holds broadcasting equipment. A 408-foot (124-m) spire points upward into the sky.

MIXING FORM AND FUNCTION

One World Trade Center's designers wanted more than just a beautiful structure. The new building had to be strong, safe, and energy efficient. It had

PERSPECTIVES
REMEMBERING AND REBUILDING

After the collapse of the Twin Towers, New Yorkers faced a difficult decision. Some people wanted to rebuild the Twin Towers. But some families of the victims did not want anything built where their loved ones had died. Eventually all sides reached an agreement. New buildings would be constructed. A memorial and museum would honor the lives that had been lost.

The tower's spire brings the building to its 1,776-foot (541-m) height.

The Twin Towers stood from their completion in 1973 until 2001.

to withstand gravity, wind, and earthquakes. It also had to be resistant to the kinds of attacks that destroyed the Twin Towers.

The team of architects and engineers designed a one-of-a-kind building. They brought concrete, steel, and glass together to create a sleek, safe skyscraper.

STRAIGHT TO THE
SOURCE

In this passage, Kenneth Lewis of the architectural firm that designed One World Trade Center discusses how light was considered during the design process:

> One World Trade Center . . . marks in the sky what is marked by the memorial pools in the ground. . . . The design team really started from a very simple premise that the building needed to be iconic in a very clear and simple way, that its form would gain its strength from reflectivity and light. . . . To capture that light we began experiments with the glass and how it reflected and captured light, both daytime and nighttime in the building. And that also went to the light inside the building. You can be up on any one of the floors on a regular day, not a particularly sunny day, and you can read a newspaper well into late in the afternoon without having any lights.

Source: "Architecture and Innovation of One World Trade Center." *9/11 Tribute Center*. YouTube, February 26, 2015. Web. Accessed November 12, 2016.

What's the Big Idea?

Take a close look at this passage. What was one of the team's goals in designing One World Trade Center? Why was capturing light an important part of the design process? How did they go about accomplishing their goal?

CHAPTER TWO

PREPARING TO BUILD A TOWER

After the September 11 tragedy, investigators studied why the Twin Towers collapsed. Engineers took another look at the effects of extreme heat and fire on steel. The exact reasons for the towers' collapses are still unknown. But engineers realized the new building needed a solid core. They used what they learned to make One World Trade Center strong and safe.

The tragedy of the September 11 attacks left the surrounding area covered in dust and debris. After it was cleaned up, people had to decide what to do with the space.

TEST MODELS

Before construction began, One World Trade Center's designers built small models of the building. They subjected the models to physical tests. The tests showed if the building was strong enough to resist different forces. Engineers successfully tested one model's resistance to explosives. They tested a model against wind and rain. They blasted it with air from an airplane propeller. They shot strong jets of water at it. Tests showed the tower could cope with high winds and driving rain.

DEVISING A DESIGN

One World Trade Center began as architects' sketches on paper. The building's designers combined art, math, and engineering to develop a plan for the structure. Architect Daniel Libeskind designed a master plan for the World Trade Center area. David Childs, an experienced skyscraper architect, also worked on the project. The final building plan used Libeskind's idea for a 1,776-foot (541-m)

Daniel Libeskind showed off an early design for the tower in December 2002.

The forces acting on a building's structure include the weight of things such as workers and office furniture.

tower with a spire. David Childs selected the building's unique shape.

Software engineers worked alongside the design team. They put together a high-tech construction plan.

On a computer screen, the design team could view the building from different angles. They used software to study the forces that would act on the building.

Skyscrapers are tall and slender. To be steady and safe, they must be built to resist several forces. These forces include gravity, wind, and earthquake activity. Gravity is the force of the building's weight pushing downward. Wind can sway the building from side to side. Earthquakes can shake the tower's foundations.

GRAVITY

The weight of the building itself is known as a dead load.

PERSPECTIVES
BETTER BUILDING CODES

Engineers must follow building codes. Codes are guidelines. They spell out basic requirements that must be followed. The requirements ensure structures will be safe. After the terrorist attacks of September 11, the government updated building codes. It wanted to ensure new buildings would be safer. The updates included wider exit stairways, better fire sprinklers, and improved emergency lighting. In 2008 US Secretary of Commerce Carlos Gutierrez noted, "The lessons learned from the tragic events of 9/11 have yielded stronger building and fire codes for a new generation of safer, more robust buildings across the nation."

It does not change. Gravity pushes downward on the structure all the time. But the weight caused by office equipment, furniture, and people can change over time. These factors are known as live loads. The building must be built strong enough to withstand both dead and live loads.

A secure building begins with a strong foundation. Deep underground, massive steel and concrete members form the substructure. The substructure spreads the weight of the building over a larger area. This means that no single spot has too much weight on it.

Above ground, steel and concrete form the main building. The steel framework is the building's skeleton. Vertical steel columns withstand compression forces caused by heavy loads pushing down on them. Horizontal beams called girders connect the columns. Loads on the girders are transferred to the supporting columns.

SURVIVING WIND AND EARTHQUAKES

Skyscrapers are vulnerable to wind forces. The wind's speed increases with height. It is tricky to plan for because wind can be unpredictable. Wind pushes against buildings and flows around them. If one side moves more than another, this can produce a twisting force called torsion. Shear is another force caused by wind and earthquakes. Shear causes a sliding motion. It makes parts of a building move in opposite directions. Both torsion and shear can make a structure twist, bend, and vibrate.

Engineers design skyscrapers to sway slightly. Steel beams are connected to columns with joints. This lets the building resist swaying loads. The flexibility reduces the danger from wind and earthquakes. However, engineers must calculate carefully. Even small amounts of sway can give people motion sickness. One World

The concrete core of One World Trade Center is a large, sturdy structure.

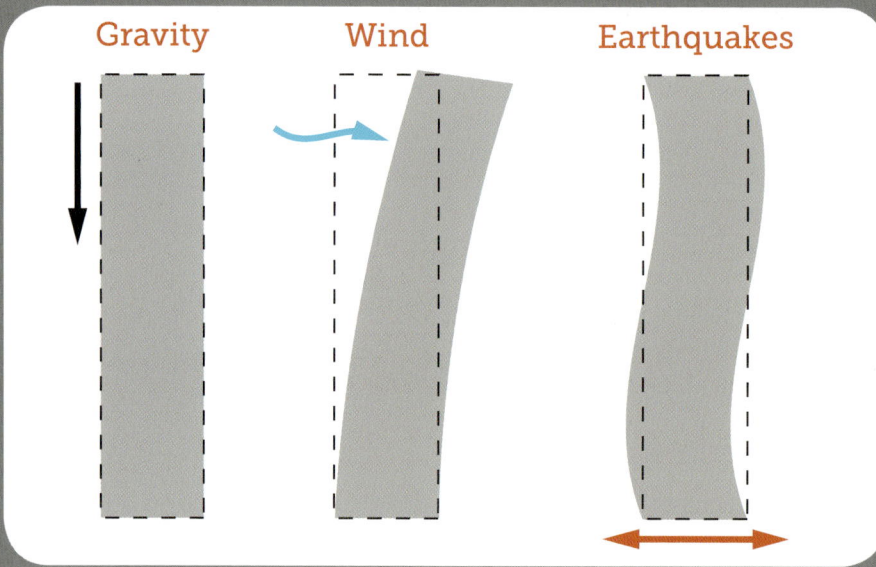

This diagram shows how the forces of gravity, wind, and earthquakes act on a building. How does a foundation help counteract gravity? What parts of a skyscraper help it withstand the force of wind and earthquakes?

Trade Center's tapered shape reduces wind force. The building's angled edges disrupt the wind's flow.

A STRONG CORE

A strong core runs along the center of the tower. The core provides support against gravity, wind, and earthquakes. One World Trade Center's core has a wall around it made from high-strength concrete. Concrete is a mixture of water, cement, and rock with sand or gravel. When it dries, the mixture becomes a sturdy building material.

Concrete comes in different strengths. Strength is measured by pounds per square inch, or psi. Standard concrete has a strength of about 3,000 to 5,000 psi. This means it can be compressed by that much force for a set period before it breaks. The core of One World Trade Center uses types of concrete with strengths of up to 14,000 psi.

FURTHER EVIDENCE

Chapter Two has information about forces that act on a skyscraper. What is the main point of this chapter? What evidence supports this point? Read the article on the website below. Does the information on the website support the main point of the chapter? What new information does it present?

HOW SKYSCRAPERS WORK: WIND RESISTANCE
abdocorelibrary.com/engineering-one-world-trade-center

CHAPTER THREE

BUILDING ONE WORLD TRADE CENTER

It took several years to design One World Trade Center. After the design was complete, the construction process started. It was carried out in stages. Work began in 2006. First, workers built the underground substructure. This portion of the tower is below ground level. Next, they put the steel frame, concrete core, and floors into place. Then they attached the curtain wall. This is a protective layer of windows around the

The building's foundation was completed in 2008.

outside of the building. Finally, they added the spire and other finishing touches.

ANCHORED TO THE GROUND

Builders began by digging down to create a secure and solid foundation. One World Trade Center's height means that there are large downward forces. This requires secure support. A deep foundation transfers the tower's dead load into the ground.

Builders dug down to reach bedrock. They secured anchors there. But before construction could continue, a big obstacle had to be overcome. Train tracks from local transit systems ran through the site. The substructure had to be built so that the tracks could run through it. Workers built a steel and concrete structure over and around the tracks.

A sturdy framework of steel forms the building's skeleton.

BLAST-PROOF BEAUTY

Above ground, the tower's superstructure is made up of 45,000 tons (40,823 metric tons) of structural steel. Beams weighing 40 tons (36 metric tons) each connect to huge, strong columns. Together, they form a massive frame. Designers knew the base of the tower, called the podium, would be vulnerable to attack. To keep it safe, the podium uses

PERSPECTIVES
COWBOYS OF THE SKY

It took more than 26,000 workers to build One World Trade Center. Workers were onsite seven days a week. Ironworkers made up a large part of the workforce. They called themselves "cowboys of the sky." These workers spent their days high above the ground. Working conditions were difficult. Temperatures high in the air could sometimes be much colder than on the ground. In the summer, days could be extremely hot. Ironworkers faced wind and storms. Sometimes workers were injured. Despite the rough conditions, workers were proud to be part of such a meaningful project.

The tower's base is built to resist attacks at ground level.

A GEOMETRIC DESIGN

One World Trade Center has a geometric design. Its base is a square. As it rises, triangular sides form an octagon at the tower's midpoint. Then, at the top, its cross section becomes a square again. What effect does this have on the appearance of the building? Do you prefer this look to a tower that is square for its entire height? Why or why not?

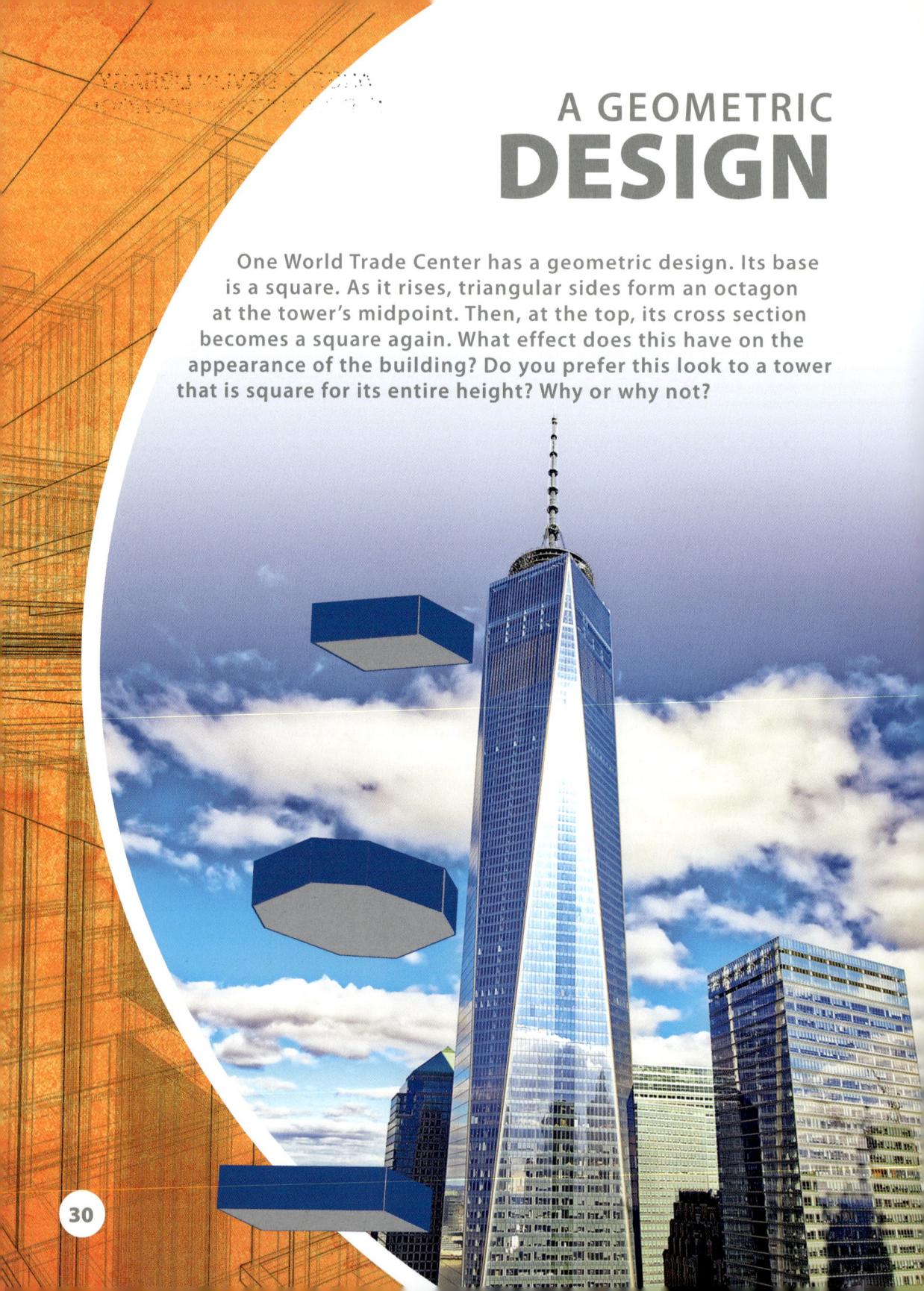

high-strength concrete and steel columns. It measures 200 feet (61 m) square and stands 187 feet (57 m) high. The podium's thick blast walls protect the building from the threat of bombs at street level.

Although the podium was secure, the design team was unhappy with the feeling it conveyed. The concrete base made the tower seem like a fortress. David Childs decided to cover the base in glass prisms. The prims would reflect light. But in testing, the glass shattered into dangerous shards. The design was changed.

SAFETY FIRST

One World Trade Center has many safety features. Elevators are located within the central concrete core. The thick concrete forms a protective barrier against fire. The core also surrounds extra wide stairways. They allow people to exit quickly. In case of fire, the stairway doors are designed to keep smoke out. One stairway is meant for use only by firefighters. This allows them to climb up the tower quickly. Concrete also protects sprinklers and other equipment.

Instead, the podium was covered in long glass slats. They were angled to allow light to pass through.

THE CORE AND THE CURTAIN WALL

One World Trade Center's core is among its most important features. The super strong spine begins below ground. It runs to the top of the tower. It is made up of concrete reinforced with steel. In some places, the core wall is almost six feet (1.8 m) thick. The concrete is fire resistant, adding an extra layer of safety. The core also houses many of the building's mechanical parts, including its 71 elevators. Five of these are express elevators. They are the country's fastest elevators. Visitors can zip from the ground to the 104th floor in a mere 60 seconds.

By 2010 tower construction was moving at one floor per week. The first 20 floors were placed in line with the square podium. After the 20th floor, the tower forms an octagon. The shape is made up of eight tapered triangles with sloping edges. The tower's curtain wall is covered in massive glass panels. Ironworkers used a hoist system to install each huge panel. They attached the panels to the steel frame. The curtain wall allows light into the building while protecting the people inside from harsh weather.

EXPLORE ONLINE

Chapter Three focuses on the construction of One World Trade Center. The article below presents some facts about building skyscrapers. How is the information from the website the same as the information in Chapter Three? What new information did you learn from the website?

SKYSCRAPERS: BUILDINGS THAT TOUCH THE SKY
abdocorelibrary.com/engineering-one-world-trade-center

CHAPTER
FOUR

ONE WORLD TRADE CENTER TODAY

One World Trade Center serves many functions. It is primarily a commercial building. This means that companies have offices there. Seventy-one of the skyscraper's 104 floors contain office space. The tower's strong steel framework allows floor space to be column-free. Floor-to-ceiling glass walls flood the large, open offices with natural light. Companies

The completed One World Trade Center has become one of New York's most famous buildings.

...ing represent many industries, including ...dvertising, and television.

...ING FOREVER

One World Trade Center stands as a symbol of strength and grace. Visitors from all around the world come to see the iconic landmark. At the nearby memorials, they pay their respects to the thousands of people who lost their lives on September 11, 2001.

At One World Trade Center, visitors can experience a spectacular view. Located on floors 100–102, One World Observatory is the tallest observation deck in the Western Hemisphere. It rises 1,268 feet (386 m) above the street. The observatory includes a theater, exhibits, and dining areas.

MAINTAINING THE TOWER

A building as complex and large as One World Trade Center requires constant upkeep. Inside the building,

Visitors to the observation deck have the highest view in New York City.

PERSPECTIVES
DANGLING DANGEROUSLY

In November 2014, two window washers were working on a scaffold outside the 68th floor. One of the platform's cables loosened. One side of the scaffold dropped. The platform dangled hundreds of feet above the ground. Luckily, the men were attached to the scaffold by cables. Even though they were terrified, they stayed calm. Rescue crews cut through a window with a diamond saw. After dangling for 90 minutes, the workers were pulled to safety.

workers keep the lobby, offices, and observatory clean. Building staff ensure the elevators, heating, and cooling run smoothly. Trained crews maintain the spire's communications and lighting equipment. They work at dizzying heights. Engineers designed special fall protection systems. Workers attach themselves with metal clips and cables to tracks on the spire. This keeps them safe as they climb.

One World Trade Center is under tight security. The tower and surrounding area are patrolled by the

Safety and security are a major focus at the One World Trade Center site.

New York City Police Department and private security guards. Cameras and other surveillance equipment take in information. Security staff keep a watchful eye on activity in the area. All visitors must pass through a security screening area.

WINNING THE GOLD

One World Trade Center received LEED (Leadership in Energy and Environmental Design) Gold certification. This award recognizes excellence in environmentally friendly construction. More than 40 percent of the tower's construction materials were made from recycled goods. The building's coated glass conserves energy. Fuel cells provide clean energy. Rainwater collected from the roof is reused. The tower uses efficient low-energy equipment.

REACHING INTO THE FUTURE

One World Trade Center took several years to complete. Architects, engineers, and builders faced many challenges. They worked together to create a magnificent and meaningful masterpiece. One World Trade Center is more than an engineering marvel. It brings people together and honors the past. It is a symbol of hope for a brighter future. One World Trade Center set a high standard for future skyscrapers. Its construction reached new heights of architectural and engineering achievement.

STRAIGHT TO THE SOURCE

In an interview, architect David Childs discussed what he found most interesting about the tower's form and structure:

> WTC 1 is a solution to many technical problems, and it represents the very best in codes, structure, and safety. It's a concrete core with steel exterior, which is an efficient and safe system. . . . The form tapers on its four corners, which buildings (like trees) want to do anyway. The original towers had such deep floors, they were psychologically oppressive. The taper solves this, and it keeps the building efficient, since we can taper the core, too. . . . One of the problems on 9/11 was a communication breakdown between first responders, so we included a radio system throughout the building.
>
> Source: John Gendall. "AIArchitect Talks with David Childs, FAIA." *American Institute of Architects*. American Institute of Architects, 2016. Web. Accessed October 23, 2016.

Point of View
What does Childs think some of the problems were with the original Twin Towers? How did he use his architectural skills to solve these problems in the new building?

FAST FACTS

- One World Trade Center was built after the destruction of the Twin Towers in the attacks of September 11, 2001.
- Architects and engineers used computer software to design and plan the tower.
- Skyscrapers must withstand the forces of gravity, wind, and earthquakes.
- One World Trade Center is made from steel, concrete, and glass.
- Skyscrapers are designed to be flexible and to sway.
- One World Trade Center's tapered shape reduces wind force.
- One World Trade Center is secured into the bedrock.
- The glass-covered podium base is blast resistant.
- The core protects the elevators, stairwells, and mechanics of the building.
- The curtain wall is covered in enormous glass panels.
- One World Trade Center requires constant maintenance and upkeep.
- One World Trade Center is rated as an environmentally friendly skyscraper.

STOP AND THINK

Surprise Me

Chapter Two discusses the forces that architects and engineers must consider before constructing a skyscraper. After reading this book, what two or three facts about building skyscrapers did you find most surprising? Write a few sentences about each fact. Why did you find each fact surprising?

Take a Stand

Many people think that supertall skyscrapers are beautiful buildings. But others believe the skyscrapers are eyesores. What do you think about skyscrapers? Do you think cities should build taller buildings? Do skyscrapers add or take away from a city's beauty? Why?

Why Do I Care?

Maybe you have never been in a skyscraper. But that doesn't mean you can't think about how buildings are designed and constructed. What kinds of buildings have you been in? What forces are acting on these buildings?

You Are There

This book discusses the building of One World Trade Center. Imagine you are on site during the construction. Write a letter home telling your friends what you observe. What parts of the building are being constructed first? How is the rising tower changing the city's skyline?

GLOSSARY

architect
a person who designs buildings

cascade
to flow or pour down

core
the central part of something

engineer
a person trained to design and build

iconic
widely recognized

software
a computer program, also called an app or application

spire
a tall tower on top of a building that comes to a point

substructure
an underground support system

symbolic
expressing an idea without using words

taper
to become smaller or thinner at one end

LEARN MORE

Books

Finger, Brad. *13 Skyscrapers Children Should Know.* New York: Prestel Publishing, 2016.

Gagne, Tammy. *Women in Engineering.* Minneapolis, MN: Abdo Publishing, 2017.

O'Keefe, Emily. *September 11 through the Eyes of George W. Bush.* Minneapolis, MN: Abdo Publishing, 2016.

Websites

To learn more about Building by Design, visit **abdobooklinks.com.** These links are routinely monitored and updated to provide the most current information available.

Visit **abdocorelibrary.com** for free additional tools for teachers and students.

INDEX

building codes, 18, 41
Burj Khalifa, 6

Childs, David, 14, 16, 31, 41
computers, 17
concrete, 10, 19, 22–23, 25, 26, 31, 32, 41
construction workers, 25, 26, 29, 33
core, 22–23, 25, 31, 32, 41
curtain wall, 25, 32–33

earthquakes, 10, 18, 21–22
elevators, 31, 32, 38

environmentally friendly construction, 40

foundation, 19, 26

gravity, 10, 18–19, 22

Lewis, Kenneth, 11
Libeskind, Daniel, 14

models, 14

observation deck, 36–38
offices, 35–36

podium, 29–32

safety features, 31
security, 38–39
shape, 30
skyscrapers, 6, 18, 21, 22
spire, 9, 16, 26, 38
substructure, 19, 25, 26
superstructure, 29

Twin Towers, 6, 9, 10, 13, 41

wind, 10, 14, 18, 21, 22
window washers, 38

About the Author

Cecilia Pinto McCarthy has written several science and nature books for children. She also teaches environmental science programs at a nature sanctuary. She lives with her family north of Boston, Massachusetts.